A Thunderstorm Is Coming!

by Margie Sigman

Strategy Focus

As you read about thunderstorms, **monitor** your understanding. If you have questions, reread to **clarify** what you did not understand.

 HOUGHTON MIFFLIN   BOSTON

Key Vocabulary

bolt a flash of lightning

horizon the line where the sky and the earth seem to meet

lightning a flash of light in the sky

rumbled made a deep, rolling sound

thunder the rumbling sound that follows lightning

weather what it is like outside

Word Teaser

Where there's thunder, there's _____.

It was a hot summer day. There were
dark clouds far away on the horizon.

Suddenly, thunder rumbled.
A thunderstorm was coming.

Thunderstorms usually have strong winds and hard rain. They can happen very quickly.

You may see lightning and hear thunder during a thunderstorm.

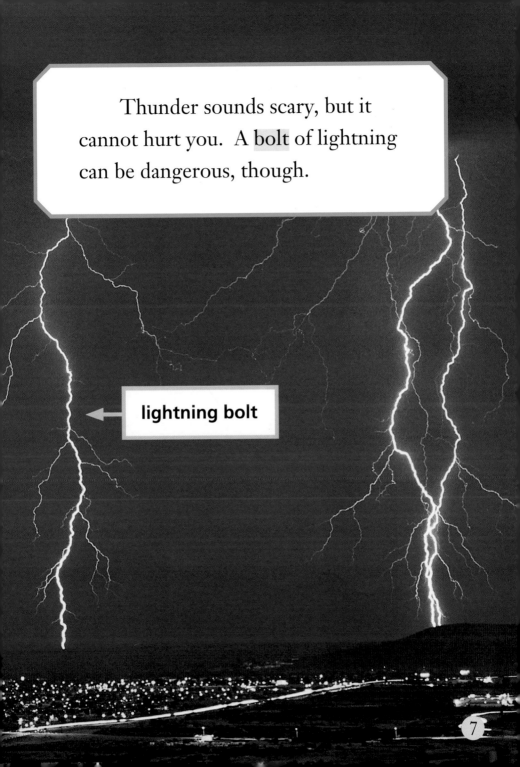

Thunder sounds scary, but it cannot hurt you. A bolt of lightning can be dangerous, though.

lightning bolt

Be careful if you see lightning.
Follow these rules if you are outdoors
and the weather looks stormy.

1. Find shelter right away.
2. If there is no safe shelter, find
   a low spot.
3. Do NOT stand under a tree.

Be careful even if you are indoors
during a thunderstorm.

Do not use the phone. Stay away
from windows.

Finally, the thunderstorm is over.
What did you do to stay safe?

NOTE

NOTE

NOTE

Putting Words to Work

1. Why are some people afraid of **thunder**? Explain your answer.

2. What is your favorite kind of **weather**?

3. Complete this sentence:
   A **bolt** of **lightning** can _____.

4. What is the first thing you should do if you see **lightning** on the **horizon**?

5. PARTNER ACTIVITY: Think of a word you learned in the text. Explain its meaning to your partner and give an example.

Answer to Word Teaser
lightning